The Ribbon Dance

By Debbie Croft
Illustrations by Christina Miesen

At school, our teacher, Ms Costa, helped my friends and me to make up a **ribbon** dance. We wanted to do it at the school concert.

Ribbon
Dancing

First, we had to get the ribbons ready
for our dance.
Ms Costa gave each one of us
a stick and a long ribbon.
She helped us to tie the ribbons
onto the end of the sticks.
My ribbon was blue
and I liked it the best.

Then, we went into the school **hall** to make up our dance.
Ms Costa played the music for us.
Sometimes, the music was slow and sometimes it was fast.
It was just right for our ribbon dance!

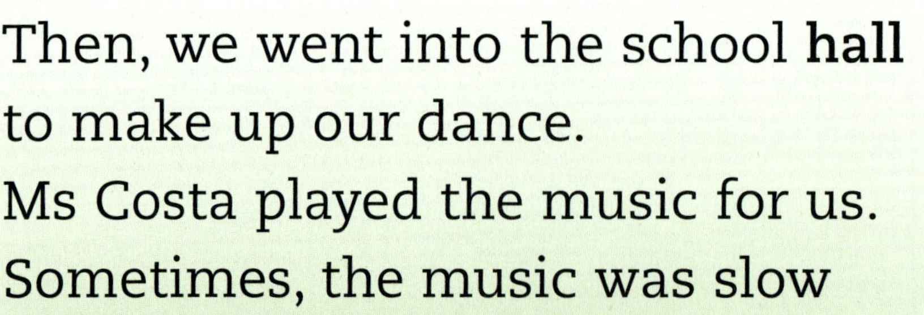

At the start, the music was slow.
We moved the ribbons
up above our heads,
and down near the floor.

Then, we made the sticks
go round and round slowly,
so the ribbons made big **circles**.

When the music got faster,
we moved the sticks
up and down very quickly.
The ribbons made little waves.

Then, we made small, fast circles
with the sticks.
And the ribbons made little circles, too.

Every day, we went into the hall at lunch time.
We tried hard to make our dance better and better.
Ms Costa said she liked our dance very much.

She told us we could wear a **leotard** when we did the dance at the concert.

At home, I had a blue leotard.
It looked good with my blue ribbon.

Lots of people came to watch the concert.

Before we started our ribbon dance,
all my friends were feeling a little bit scared.
But when the music began,
we danced out onto the stage.

We moved our ribbons in circles and waves in time with the music.

I looked down and saw my family.
Everyone was clapping and smiling.
I was very happy with our dance.

Glossary

circles round shapes

hall a big room

leotard a dancer's clothing

ribbon a long strip of cloth